MR. BRAVE

Roger Hargreaves

Original concept by
Roger Hargreaves

This is a story about Mr Brave.

Now, Mr Brave is not as strong as Mr Strong.

And he is not as tall as Mr Tall.

But, as you will soon see, that does not stop him being brave.

This story happened last Tuesday, when Little Miss Bossy rang Mr Brave to invite him to tea.

"AND DON'T BE LATE!" she shouted down the phone.

It was a very stormy day, but Mr Brave knew that Little Miss Bossy's temper was worse.

So, he set off for Little Miss Bossy's house, hurrying along as fast as he could, to be sure that he was not late for tea.

Along the way he heard a cry for help.

It was Mr Messy.

He had been blown into the river by the wind.

Mr Brave did not want to be late for Little Miss Bossy.

But, being the brave fellow he was, he jumped into the river and rescued Mr Messy.

"Oh thank you," said Mr Messy. "You're so brave, Mr Brave."

Wet right through, Mr Brave hurried on along the lane.

Suddenly, he heard somebody sobbing loudly.

Who could it be?

It was Little Miss Somersault!

She was balancing on a tightrope tied between two tall trees!

"Oh, Mr Brave, I'm so lonely," she sobbed. "Nobody will come and play on my tightrope! They are all too frightened of heights."

"You're so brave, Mr Brave," she added. "Won't you come and join me?"

Mr Brave looked up at Little Miss Somersault.

He did not want to be late for Little Miss Bossy.

But, being the brave fellow he was, he took pity on Little Miss Somersault and climbed up on to the tightrope.

They chatted away happily for a while, until Mr Brave happened to look down.

"Little Miss Somersault! Look!" he cried out in panic. "The rope is going to snap! We're going to fall … and it's such a long way down. Oh calamity! Oh help!"

"Be brave, Mr Brave," said Little Miss Somersault.

And, without more ado, she carried him safely back down to the ground.

"Oh thank you," said Mr Brave, with a sigh of relief.

Little Miss Somersault said goodbye.

And left Mr Brave on his own, shaking like a leaf.

"I don't deserve to be called Mr Brave," he said to himself. "I was scared stiff! Thank goodness nobody knows my secret."

And nobody does know his secret.

Or do they?

Now, Little Miss Trouble just happened to be passing, and she had seen and heard everything.

And what she had seen and heard had given her an idea.

A very naughty idea!

She grinned a mischievous grin.

"Hey, come here, everybody," she shouted at the top of her voice. "Come and see this!"

Very quickly a large crowd gathered.

"I have an announcement," announced
Little Miss Trouble.

"Did you know that Mr Brave isn't brave at all?"

"No, it can't be true," said the crowd, all together.

"It is true!" said Little Miss Trouble. "And I'll prove it
to you."

"Mr Brave," she continued, "I dare you to walk across that tightrope!"

Mr Brave looked up at the tightrope.

And all the crowd looked up at the tightrope.

Then all the crowd looked at Mr Brave.

Mr Brave suddenly remembered something.

A very important something.

"Just look at the time!" he said. "I'm going to be late for tea at Little Miss Bossy's!"

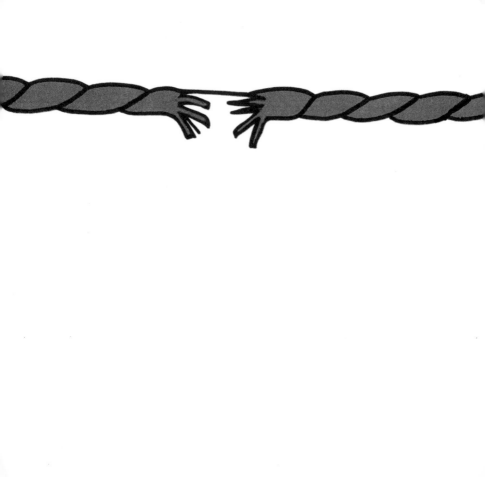

"Must dash!" he cried.

And he ran off as quickly as possible.

"Hooray!" cheered the crowd.

And they all clapped and applauded Mr Brave.

Little Miss Trouble looked puzzled.

"Why are you cheering him?" she cried. "He ran away! He isn't brave at all!"

"Oh yes, he is!" they all shouted. "Would you turn up late for tea at Little Miss Bossy's?"

Little Miss Trouble thought for a moment.

"Gosh!" she said in awe. "He is brave after all!"